Puppy Mudge
Has a Snack

Puppy Mudge Has a Snack

By Cynthia Rylant

Illustrated by Isidre Mones
in the style of Suçie Stevenson

READY-TO-READ

ALADDIN PAPERBACKS
New York   London   Toronto   Sydney

First Aladdin Paperbacks edition June 2004

Text copyright © 2003 by Cynthia Rylant
Illustrations copyright © 2003 by Suçie Stevenson

ALADDIN PAPERBACKS
An imprint of Simon & Schuster Children's Publishing Division
1230 Avenue of the Americas
New York, NY 10020

READY-TO-READ is a registered trademark of Simon & Schuster.

Book design by Mark Siegel
The text of this book was set in Goudy.
The illustrations are rendered in pen-and-ink and watercolor.
Printed in the United States of America
10 9 8 7 6 5 4 3 2 1

Also available in a Simon & Schuster Book for Young Readers hardcover edition.

The Library of Congress has cataloged the hardcover edition as follows:
Rylant, Cynthia.
Puppy Mudge has a snack / by Cynthia Rylant ; illustrated by Suçie Stevenson.
p. cm.
Summary: When Henry has a snack, his puppy Mudge wants one too.
ISBN 0-689-83981-2 (hc.)
[1. Dogs—Fiction. 2. Animals—Infancy—Fiction. 3. Snack foods—Fiction.]
I. Stevenson, Suçie, ill. II. Title
PZ7.R982Hllf 2001
[E]—dc21
00-052240
ISBN 0-689-86995-9 (Aladdin pbk.)

This is Mudge.

He is Henry's puppy.

Mudge wants Henry's snack.

"No, Mudge," says Henry.

Mudge gets on Henry's lap.

"No, Mudge," says Henry.

Mudge wants Henry's snack.

Mudge gets on Henry's head.

"No, Mudge," says Henry.

Mudge wants Henry's snack.

Mudge drools.

"Aw, Mudge," says Henry.

Mudge looks cute.

Mudge looks very, very cute.

Mudge looks too cute.

"Mudge, you are TOO cute,"
says Henry.

Henry gets a snack for Mudge.
It is a CRACKER.

Mudge LOVES crackers.

Now Henry has a snack.
And Mudge has a snack.

And all Mudge had to be was
CUTE!